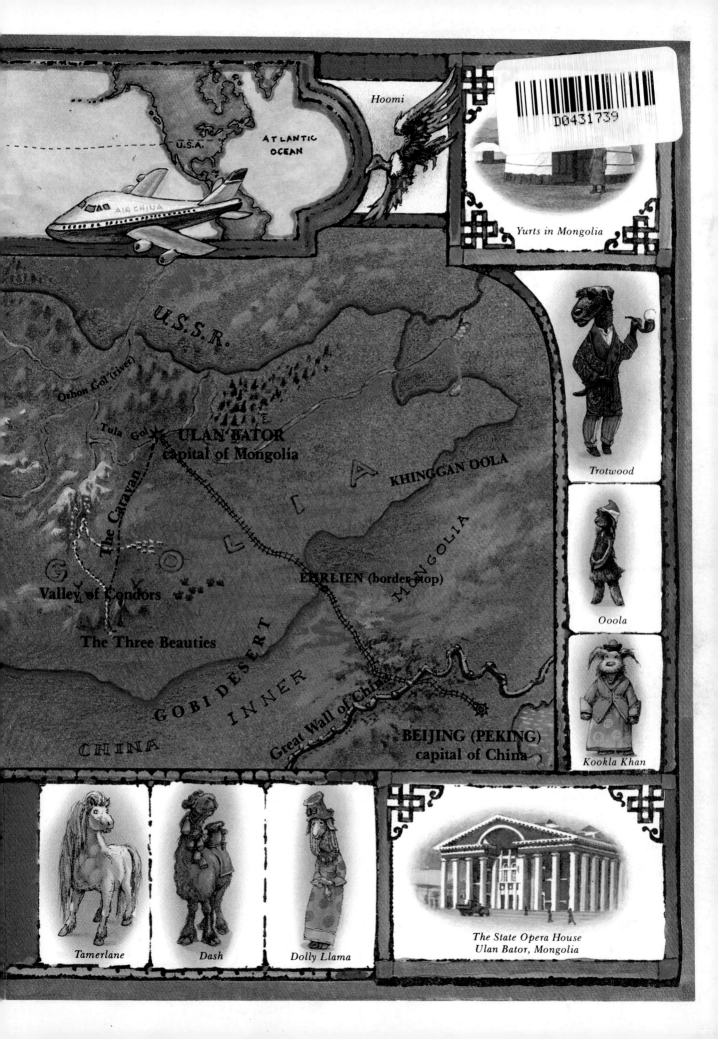

Hoomi

U.S.A.

ATLANTIC OCEAN

AIR CHINA

Yurts in Mongolia

U.S.S.R.

Orhon Gol (river)

Tula Gol

ULAN BATOR
capital of Mongolia

The Caravan

KHINGGAN OOLA

Trotwood

Valley of Condors

EHRLIEN (border stop)

MONGOLIA

Ooola

The Three Beauties

INNER

G O B I   D E S E R T

CHINA

Great Wall of China

BEIJING (PEKING)
capital of China

Kookla Khan

Tamerlane

Dash

Dolly Llama

The State Opera House
Ulan Bator, Mongolia

Miss Baba IN

THE **DOORKNOB** OF

DESTINY

Winslow Pels & Richard Pels

Illustrated by
Winslow Pels

A CALICO BOOK

Published by Contemporary Books, Inc.
CHICAGO · NEW YORK

Library of Congress Cataloging-in-Publication Data
Pels, Winslow, 1947–
Miss Baba in The doorknob of destiny.
"A Calico book."
Bibliography: p.
Summary: Miss Baba, a pedigreed poodle and amateur
detective, journeys with an animal entourage to remote
Mongolia to help a canine foundling discover the secret
of her birthright.
[1. Dogs—Fiction.   2. Animals—Fiction.   3. Mongolia
—Fiction.   4. Mystery and detective stories]   I. Pels,
Richard.   II. Title.   III. Title: Doorknob of destiny.
PZ7.P3663Do   1989   [Fic]   89-802
ISBN 0-8092-4401-2

*For Joshua, Dianne, Linus, Lily, Tom, Mark, Mary, Miles,
Stephan, Dennis, Helaine, Al, Yolanda, Li, Fan, Ye Lin, Galsan,
Joe, Bob, Esther, Joan, Bob, Michael, Peter, Julie, Harriet, and
everyone else who helped Miss Baba get to Mongolia and back.*

*A portion of the proceeds from the sale of this book will be
donated to the World Wildlife Fund.*

CONTENTS

AUTHORS' NOTE

While the geography and local color of *The Doorknob of Destiny* are substantially correct, any resemblance between the characters of this book and real people is purely coincidental and quite remarkable.

CAST OF CHARACTERS

MISS BABA FURBELOW   A prim poodle in a stylish fried-egg hat. Founder of Miss Baba's Animal Academy and Traveling Theatre, a foundling home in Ballston Spa, New York. She's a take-charge kind of poodle with a nose for adventure.

OOOLA   Young Ooola was found in the most approved fashion for foundlings, on the doorstep. Now a teenager, she is determined to unravel her past.

TROTWOOD   Miss Baba's dapper cousin and occasional director of the Traveling Theatre. Among his passions are frequent meals and chess.

PROFESSOR NOD   A woolly yak who specializes in ancient Asian languages, most of them extinct, and is an avid chess player.

MISS MARVA UPTIGRUE   Professor Nod's protective secretary.

ANIMAL MARIA   Cook for the foundling home. A true artist in the kitchen—is it any wonder that the sumptuous production of *Aïda* is left in her capable paws?

NURSE PINCHER   Head of the dispensary at the Animal Academy. She administers remedies and vaccinations when necessary.

DIMCHUCK   The not-so-dim camel driver and guide.

TAMERLANE   The leader of the White Stallions, with service to the khan in his bloodlines.

DOLLY LLAMA   A llama, an animal native to South America. She is also a lama, a great teacher and spiritual leader who has spent her life studying ancient historical and religious manuscripts. She is familiar with history, legend, and lore. Dolly is probably the only llama in Mongolia, but not the only lama.

KOOKLA KHAN   Which is she—a true Mongolian royalty or a mongrel princess?

DASH   An evil-smelling camel with an even worse disposition.

EGAD & HOOMI   Condors who are willing, if not happy, to repay a favor.

LUCILLE   Ooola's understudy in the Traveling Theatre. She stars in *Aïda* while Ooola searches for her past.

The foundlings made way for a blaze of candles atop a towering pink fantasy...

CHAPTER ONE

The Birthday Party

"Oh, my dears, how glorious!" sighed Miss Baba.

Shadows danced across the porch in the late afternoon twilight. The foundlings made way for a blaze of candles atop a towering pink fantasy.

Animal Maria staggered under the weight of an eleven-layer Strawberry Dream Cake. It was her first attempt at this most difficult of cakes since she had learned the secrets of its recipe from her mentor, the Turkish master Chef Tetelli. The cook was especially proud of it.

As you might imagine, there were quite a few birthdays at Miss Baba's Animal Academy, but this one was particularly special. Ooola was close to graduation, and this was her last birthday as a student at the Academy. (As with most foundlings, her birthdate was not known for sure but was approximated.)

"Umms" and "ahs" greeted the creamy confection in Animal Maria's arms. It was decked with garlands of real scooting shimmies and filled with potato cream custard, a good deal of which would end up on the paws and faces of the appreciative company.

As the cake was carefully maneuvered onto the table, all eyes turned to Ooola, the poodle of the hour. She practiced her pucker a few times before she blew out the elaborate arrangement of candles.

Ooola slowly unwrapped all that was left of her past...

Finally the cake was cut. It was agreed that the jiggly dessert tasted as good as it looked. Nevertheless, Trotwood, Ooola's adopted uncle, required several large samplings before he could decide whether or not the consistency of the delicate potato custard filling was perfect.

"It reminds me a great deal of the Turkish Towering Inferno Cake. Yes, a great deal," remarked Trot.

Everyone contributed to make Ooola's party a gala event. The neighbors, Harriet and Leonard Westdale, had donated a croquet set from their new croquet factory in Ballston Spa. They all played a rousing match. The guests helped themselves to cheese toast and lemonade from a cart brought around by Tap Tap the donkey and Kernel Gluepots, the globe-trotting goose who recently settled down to a catering business. (While Animal Maria was a whiz at extravagant desserts like Strawberry Dream Cake, she fell completely apart when it came to something as simple and inartistic as cheese toast.)

Trotwood played "Happy Birthday" three times on the oud with a tail feather graciously donated by Gluepots. Ooola opened her presents, which included a diary, a pink wallet, an ankle bracelet, and a camera. Then Miss Baba put her paw around Ooola's shoulder and called for silence.

"Some years ago, my dear Ooola," she began, "you were left on this very doorstep, wrapped in a colorful carpet and howling for all you were worth." Miss Baba's nose moistened at the memory.

"Tied to your small, defenseless paw was a leather pouch, branded with four horseshoes and a feather. It contained an object of uncertain origin but of obvious value. Now that you're on the brink of adulthood, this occasion seems most appropriate for the return of these clues to your heritage," said Miss Baba, handing Ooola a lumpy package wrapped in brown paper. It had been wiped off, but the dust from years of sitting on a shelf remained in some of the folds. Ooola slowly unwrapped all that was left of her past.

The foundlings crowded around as Ooola unfolded an exotically woven felt rug and spread it on her lap. With trembling paws, she opened the pouch and took out the most fabulous ring any of them had ever seen. Ooola was mystified. She examined the huge, luminescent orb set in an eleven-pointed silver star.

Ooola tried to puzzle out the words engraved inside the band of the antique ring. Miss Baba came to her assistance. "It looks to me like Arabic writing, or maybe Sanskrit. Tomorrow I think we should take it to Professor Nod at the Museum of Animal Arts."

"Good man, that Professor Nod," said Trotwood between bites of potato custard and cheese toast. "Heck of a chess player."

The most fabulous ring any of them had ever seen...

"Suit yourself," said Miss Uptigrue, and returned to the book she was devouring...

CHAPTER TWO

Very Important Work

Miss Baba and Ooola made a trip the next morning to the Museum of Animal Arts, overlooking Foots Pond at the intersection of Forest Park and Fairground Avenue. In the museum's huge entrance room was a giant diorama of Ballston Spa as it looked thirty million years ago. Dogasauruses, pterodactyls, assorted trilobites, and other creatures milled around what was now a shopping mall. The two prim poodles went to the reception desk in the middle of the cavernous room and asked the information clerk for directions to Professor Nod's office.

They found it in a musty old corner of the museum, where they were greeted by the steely stare of one "Miss Marva Uptigrue" (for that was what the nameplate on her desk read). Miss Uptigrue looked up from the book she was devouring.

At the still center of the clutter was a
furry fellow in a moth-eaten suit...

"May I help you?" she asked in a tone of voice that was clearly unhelpful.

"Yes indeed," said Miss Baba. "We're here to see Professor Nod."

Miss Uptigrue peered over the large and scraggy bouquet of pfister blossoms, whose cabbage aroma pervaded the reception room. "Professor Nod is a busy man," she stated. "He is engaged in Very Important Work. There's no telling when he'll be free." She began flipping through a dog-eared desk calendar. "Perhaps next April."

Miss Baba spoke with Ooola in a whisper, then turned to Miss Uptigrue. "We will just wait here until he leaves. It's a personal and pressing matter."

"Suit yourself," said Miss Uptigrue, "but sometimes he doesn't come out for weeks." She then returned to her book, which Miss Baba noticed was entitled *Nanny and the Professor*. On its cover was splashed a picture of a square-jawed professor removing the spectacles from his earnest assistant. Miss Baba smiled and took out her knitting.

She was knitting a particularly beautiful pot holder for Animal Maria, one with a steaming tuna casserole design on it. So Miss Baba didn't mind waiting too much. Ooola, however, soon became restless. Miss Uptigrue was once again immersed in her book, and Ooola decided to walk down the hall and see what she could see.

A door was slightly ajar. Ooola peeked in. She held her breath, expecting to see someone unwrapping a mummy or perhaps a room full of hungry spiders. But what she saw was a room that was floor to ceiling with piles of books, some of which had spilled out in unsteady-looking drifts. In the calm center of the clutter was a furry fellow in a moth-eaten suit, sitting at a chess table, with his back to her.

"Excuse me," said Ooola. There was no movement, so she repeated, rather loudly, "Excuse me!"

Professor Nod woke with a start, almost knocking over the chess board. *"What is it?"* he cried out. "I thought my lecture wasn't until Thursday. This is only . . . only, umm, Monday?"

"No sir, it's Friday. And I'm not here for your lecture, though I would very much like to hear it," replied Ooola. "I have a ring that has an inscription I would like you to translate for me."

Nod blinked and fumbled in his jacket pockets for his glasses. Putting them on, he studied Ooola for a moment, then smiled. "What is your name, young lady?"

At that moment Miss Baba peered around the edge of the door. Professor Nod looked over at her and said, "Well, this office is a regular Grand Central Station today, isn't it? Now who might you be, Madam? Wait, we've met, haven't we? At one of those museum fund-raisers? You're Miss Thingamabob."

"Miss Baba Furbelow, Professor. And this is my ward, Ooola. I hope she didn't disturb you."

9

"The horseshoes, the feather, those are the postmarks of the khans..."

"Not at all," he fibbed. "Now what's all this about a ring?"

Ooola handed him the carpet and the pouch containing the ring. Nod lingered over the carpet. His hoof ran across the intricate patterns and creatures and symbols woven into its fabric. He turned to his anxious guests and said, "I can't make out the message of this carpet, but these patterns certainly mean something. *The Secret History of the Mongols* might have something about it. I'll make a note to myself to do some research. But it's definitely very old and probably quite valuable."

Ooola asked excitedly, "What about the ring, Professor?"

He picked up the ancient leather pouch and examined the symbols painted on it. "The horseshoes and the feather are the postmarks of the khans, the former rulers of Mongolia. This pattern was a particular favorite of Chingis Khan, I might add."

He put out his hoof and dropped the ring into the cleft. "Now, what's this?" he asked himself. The professor turned the ring in the light. He put a jeweler's magnifying glass to his eye and looked at all the details of the ring, including the inscription. By now all traces of sleepiness had left him. The excitement in his features made him seem years younger. Nod read the inscription slowly and deliberately:

"In the Valley of Condors, grasp the Doorknob of Destiny."

At that moment a curled horn appeared at the door, followed closely by the head of a grumpy Miss Uptigrue, her wattles quivering with indignation. She took Ooola by the paw and began leading her out of the office. Miss Uptigrue clucked, "He doesn't like being disturbed. I told you he is extremely busy. Very Important Work."

Professor Nod interjected, "Miss Uptigrue, it's all right. I was just taking a moment from my busy schedule to help Miss Furbelly and the young lady . . ."

Miss Uptigrue smiled. "That's just like him—so much to do and he still is willing to overextend himself just to help any stranger who happens to sneak in unannounced."

Over her shoulder Ooola managed to ask one last question of the illustrious and well-guarded professor. "What am I supposed to do with the ring?"

"I don't know," the professor called back, "but the Valley of Condors is in the Gobi Desert. That's in Mongolia! If you decide to go there, let me know. I've been planning an expedition there myself . . ."

With that Miss Uptigrue very firmly and not too politely showed Ooola and Miss Baba the door.

They gathered at the front door with their luggage for one last check...

CHAPTER THREE

Passage to Peking

There are some places in the world one can just decide to visit, pack a toothbrush, buy a plane ticket, and, within hours, be there. Mongolia is not one of those places. Miss Baba and Ooola found this out very quickly. To go to Mongolia, one needs permission from a Mongolian embassy. There's one in China, one in the Soviet Union, but none in the United States. It takes at least two months even to apply for a visa. The travel agent in Ballston Spa tried to convince them to go to Saskatchewan instead.

Then Miss Baba thought of the Traveling Theatre, a project she had begun at her Animal Academy several years earlier. Recently Trotwood had been coaching twelve of the children (including Ooola) in a full-costume production of the famous opera *Aïda*. In rehearsal they sounded quite good.

Miss Baba called Trotwood and ran her idea by him. Trotwood was delighted. "Baba, old bean, taking the Traveling Theatre to the capital of Mongolia! A capital idea! We'll knock them dead, so to speak, with a first-rate production of *Aïda*."

Poster for the full-costume production of
the famous opera, Aïda.

Miss Baba was pleased by Trot's enthusiasm. She added, "I talked to the Metropolitan Opera, and they're interested in arranging an exchange program that will cut through all the red tape. They'll have all our papers ready for us in a week or two. The Mongolian Opera will perform the Mongolian classic *The Three Fateful Hills* in New York, and Miss Baba's Animal Academy and Traveling Theatre will perform *Aïda* in the Mongolian State Opera House in Ulan Bator. By the way, the director of the Metropolitan Opera asked me to say hello to you."

"Good fellow! And Baba, old bean, you know this will be a huge undertaking. I'll need help. Can I borrow Animal Maria? She'll make a splendid assistant stage manager." Trot was thinking of Animal Maria's way with desserts as much as her way with children.

Ooola was beside herself with excitement. After one rehearsal (she was coaching her understudy, Lucille), she happened to mention to Trotwood, "It's a shame we can't coordinate our trip with Professor Nod's. He said he was going to Mongolia. But to get by that Miss Uptigrue! Forget it."

Trot's ears perked up. "Actually, that's a fine idea. I'll mention it to Professor Nod tonight at the Chess Club. Heck of a chess player, that Nod."

The following week of preparations was a busy one. First Nurse Pincher gave the twelve foundlings going on the trip inoculations for typhoid, cholera, and yellow fever. The shots

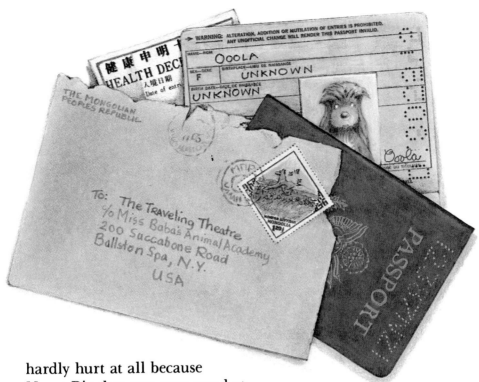

hardly hurt at all because
Nurse Pincher was very good at
giving them (she always practiced on oranges beforehand).

The day of departure arrived, and Miss Baba had the
Traveling Theatre, Trotwood, Professor Nod, and Animal Maria
gathered at the front door with their luggage for one last check
that they had everything they needed—including the scenery and
props for *Aïda*. They said their excited good-byes to the
remaining thirty-five foundlings and to Nurse Pincher, whose
job it was to look after them. With that they piled into the
school bus and lumbered off for Kennedy Airport.

After three hours spent checking their luggage, they
boarded an Air China jumbo jet and settled in for almost a full
day and night in the air.

Luckily Miss Baba had planned some diversions to break
the monotony of the twenty-hour trip. She had instructed
Animal Maria to whip up plenty of Traveling Hip Dips for
everyone to munch on. And during the flight they saw two
movies. Their favorite was about the Mongolian Circus. It
starred a glamorous contortionist who could twist her body in
almost any direction, as well as several famous goats and yaks
who could walk tightropes, survive being blown from a cannon,

15

It starred a glamorous contortionist who could twist her body in almost any direction...

drive motorcycles through fire, and spin dozens of plates on long
sticks. Young Lefty tried this last trick in the airplane.
Fortunately all the plates he used were plastic.

At dinnertime they were served "whole pigeon soup," an
unforgettable dish with the pigeon's feet sticking straight up out
of the broth. "I'm glad Gluepots isn't here to see this," whispered
Trotwood to Miss Baba. Animal Maria asked for the recipe.

The pilot announced over the loudspeaker system a message
in Chinese, which Professor Nod understood and Trotwood
understood somewhat. Then the pilot translated his message into
English. "We are about to land in Beijing, also known as
Peking, the capital of China. If you look out the windows on
the left, you'll see the city."

It was evening in China. But unlike New York City, which
is ablaze with light every night, Beijing had only a few lights
flickering here and there in the hills.

When they landed, they were all a little stiff and glad to be
on solid ground again. Everyone looked forward to sleeping in a
train berth instead of an airplane seat. Ooola was even more

excited than the rest of them. She was so close to the land of her ancestors!

While Animal Maria watched the tired youngsters and their baggage, Miss Baba and Trotwood navigated their way through the crowds and confusion of the airport and found a friendly horse with a cart large enough to carry them all. Professor Nod, who was busy sorting out everyone's passports, visas, and train tickets, had given Miss Baba a piece of paper on which was carefully written in Chinese, "Take us to the train station, please." She showed it to the horse.

He read it, smiled, and delivered a very long, complicated answer in Chinese. From his smile and gestures Miss Baba gathered that he had agreed to their request, so she smiled and nodded back at the fellow. It seemed she was right, because before long they were on the train and on their way to Mongolia.

Whole pigeon soup

Ooola and Miss Baba took a picture from the back of the train with Ooola's birthday camera...

CHAPTER FOUR

The Trans-Mongolian Railway

The overnight train to Mongolia was at the station and ready to leave when Miss Baba's Traveling Theatre arrived. They sleepily piled into their compartments and went to bed without even changing into their pajamas.

But fatigue didn't keep the foundlings from waking with the first light of dawn. From that moment on, they kept their noses pressed to the windows (except when Animal Maria was wiping off the smudges). The train sped along, going north, then west. They went through a tunnel under the Great Wall of China which zigzagged across the mountains for two thousand miles. Ooola and Miss Baba took a picture from the back of the train with Ooola's birthday camera.

Miss Baba shared some interesting pieces of information with the children. "The Great Wall was built two thousand years ago to repel the ancestors of the people we are going to visit, the Mongols. Today the Great Wall is the only structure on Earth that astronauts can see from the moon."

Professor Nod scribbled a note to himself about seeing the Great Wall from the moon and stuffed it into his jacket pocket.

Beyond the wall the towering gray-green mountains gave way to gentler slopes, terraced farmland, and clusters of mud-brick houses in fields of nodding sunflowers.

The countryside grew increasingly flat and turned into

grasslands dotted with herds of camels, yaks, horses, sheep, and cows and then into rocky yellow plains. This was the beginning of the Gobi Desert, which isn't a sand desert, but rather an endless expanse of dirt and rock covered with tough, leathery plants that probably could grow anywhere.

About midday the Traveling Theatre visited the dining car, where they were served pancakes stuffed with curds and cups full of hot cocoa. "The cocoa's a nice touch," commented Trot after his third helping.

Every now and then a lone horse appeared by the tracks holding a yellow train signal in his mouth. That was the "all clear" sign, and the train sped on.

When night came and it was too dark to see anything out the windows, the tired foundlings piled into their berths, covering themselves with thick, woolly green blankets handed out by the conductors. Miss Baba, Trotwood, Animal Maria, and Professor Nod stayed up and played chess for a while. Finally they too tucked themselves in. (Animal Maria had asked for two blankets.)

Just when everyone was sound asleep, lulled by the rhythmic chugging of the train, a blaring rendition of something that sounded like "Jingle Bells" blasted inexplicably over the loudspeaker. The train came to a screeching halt.

They kept their noses pressed to the windows...

Ooola blinked. *"Jingle Bells"?* The lights went on in her compartment, and she was surprised to see a gangly Chinese conductor with dark glasses and a goatee looking through her luggage. "What's going on?" she asked in alarm.

"Customs," said the conductor, slipping back into the hall.

"I think it's a terrible custom," said Ooola sleepily.

Everyone was awake by now and milling around. Miss Baba told them to have their passports, visas, and luggage ready to be inspected. "This is the Chinese-Mongolian border," she explained.

Suddenly the train began to rise in the air. Animal Maria held on to the table. Miss Baba looked out the window. The train was at least ten feet off the ground.

Professor Nod smiled. "Don't worry, my dears. They are merely changing the wheels from Chinese to Mongolian."

"Do they do this every time?" asked Miss Baba.

"Oh yes," he replied, "but don't worry. It takes only four hours. The rails are different sizes in China and Mongolia so that the two countries can't invade each other by train."

"That's nice," said Animal Maria.

During those four hours officials checked passports and customs officers examined everyone's luggage. They were all

Just when everyone was sound asleep, the train came to a screeching halt...

21

given a stamp on an official-looking document proclaiming that their luggage had passed inspection. Even the props for the opera were okayed.

When the officials got to Ooola's bags, there was nothing out of the ordinary in them. But Ooola was shocked to see that they were no longer neatly packed; they were a shambles. Someone had rummaged through them. *But for what?* She quickly checked to see if her camera was still there. It was. Then she thought about the ring and carpet. *Still there too*, she sighed with relief, while the inspector was saying, "Very messy job of packing, young lady. Very messy."

Just to be safe, Ooola decided to borrow a ribbon from Lucille and hang the ring around her neck.

The Mongolian wheels were finally bolted on, and the train was once again on its way. They continued on their route across the eastern Gobi Desert, which toward midday gave way to a range of gray-green hills and mountains.

As the train neared Ulan Bator, the capital city, a group of riders on white reindeer raced along the tracks, waving their hats. They were all smiling, even the reindeer.

Ulan Bator, their destination, turned out to be fairly small for a capital city and mostly paved over with concrete. It was made to look smaller by the surrounding mountains, which stretched out as far as the eye could see in every direction.

At the train station they were picked up by the director of the State Opera. *"San bainoo!"* he sang out in greeting. He shook paws all around and escorted the visitors with their own mountain—of baggage—to his motorcycle and an army-surplus truck. Trotwood rode in the motorcycle sidecar so he could talk to the director about the Traveling Theatre's production of *Aïda*.

Everyone agreed that the State Opera House was very impressive. It was huge and stood in the center of a bare concrete plaza. The building itself was painted brick red, so it stood out on the flat expanse like a cardinal in a field of snow. Inside the theater they were greeted by the stage hands, who helped unpack the props and scenery.

When evening fell, they went to their hotel. It was the second best one in Ulan Bator, which meant it was the second best in all of Mongolia. It was a tall concrete tower that looked like it was made of pink sugar cubes, and it too was surrounded by a plaza of gray concrete.

The children decided to wait until morning to unpack. When Ooola opened her suitcase to get her toothbrush, to her chagrin she found her things in a shambles again. *Either I'm getting a lot sloppier than I thought, or someone's been going through my things,* she thought. But maybe it was her imagination, because once again nothing was missing. The carpet was unrolled and the pouch was untied. She felt for the ring, now safely on the ribbon around her neck.

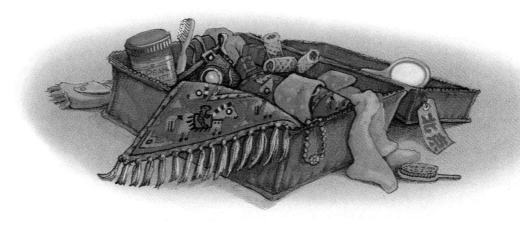

A peaceful camaraderie settled over the group...

CHAPTER FIVE

In the Shadow of Zadagag

Meanwhile Miss Baba and Professor Nod were busy with preparations for their trip with Ooola, south into the desert. They arranged to join a caravan headed for a place so few outsiders had ever seen, it wasn't even on most maps: the Valley of Condors.

Trotwood had no intention of being left behind. For the last week he'd been drilling Animal Maria with the details of every scene of the Traveling Theatre's production of *Aïda*. She had become a very capable assistant stage manager.

"Why, Animal Maria, you never told me you were such an inspired theatrical producer. You have undoubtedly directed professionally before," said Trotwood. Animal Maria blushed from her chubby ankles to her bonbon of a nose. Secretly she had always felt she had a flair for the dramatic.

Trotwood wished Animal Maria luck and then slipped off into the night. He threw a *del*, the thick woolen coat of the Mongolians, over his dapper clothes and put on the hat of an Urga camel driver. He prepared to intercept the caravan traveling south.

"Wang ba dan," hissed the large creature...

As luck would have it, right outside the hotel Miss Baba had found a very helpful guide who was part of the caravan going to the Valley of Condors. By happy coincidence the guide also spoke some English. His name was Dimchuck the Camel Driver.

At dawn the next day Miss Baba, Ooola, and Professor Nod were packed and ready. Dimchuck was waiting outside the hotel with his camel, whom he introduced as Dash. Dimchuck commanded Dash to kneel and helped the two ladies onto the camel's back, along with their luggage and Dimchuck's assorted packs.

They hadn't gone more than a mile or two when a tall, dark character in simple desert garb approached. The stranger began speaking what Nod observed was a very poor rendering of an obscure Kuldja (northwestern Chinese) dialect.

"May I join your expedition, kind sir?" Nod translated.

Dimchuck was not so polite: "Go away. Strangers are bad luck. Find your own way."

After a few exchanges like this one, the stranger removed his *del* and hat and revealed himself as none other than Trotwood.

"What trick is this? Are you joking on me?" asked a confused Dimchuck. Miss Baba assured him the joke was on her.

The camel driver accepted her explanation, but the camel had

26

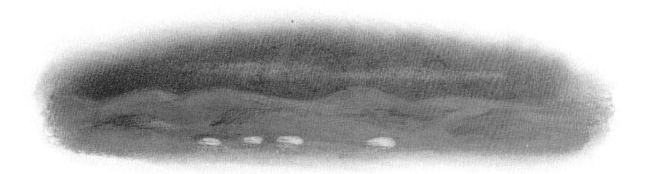

already developed a dislike for Trotwood. *"Wang ba dan,"* hissed the large creature towering over Trotwood.

"What did he say, old bean?" asked Trot.

Professor Nod replied, "He called you a turtle egg, a great insult."

"Well, do all camels act like this, or should I take it personally?" asked Trot.

"Oh, it's very personal. It doesn't take much to anger a camel, and once you do, I would forget about making friends with him," assured Nod.

By midday they had joined the caravan and were on their way into the heart of the Gobi Desert. Ooola and Miss Baba rode Dash, who walked at a remarkably slow pace (in direct contradiction to his name). Miss Baba noticed something curious sticking out of the large, loose pocket in Dimchuck's *del*—a copy of *Nanny and the Professor.* "I had no idea it had such . . . international popularity," she remarked.

Dimchuck looked displeased but managed a polite "Yes, yes."

They made camp for the evening at the base of the Flaming Cliffs of Zadagag. The camels lounged around, shifting their big, squashy feet in the sand and chewing on tufts of the leathery onionlike plants that cover the desert, which produce the distinctive odor known as "camel breath."

Dark blue felt tents with colorful good-luck charms painted all over them were quickly pitched. Dimchuck pulled the locking peg from his pack, and it tumbled from Dash's back. As he unwrapped and assembled his own tent, his eyes kept wandering off in the direction of Ooola and Professor Nod.

Miss Baba, Ooola, and the professor waved to a group of Tibetans nearby. In response these travelers from the far south stuck out their tongues. Miss Baba's eyes widened. "What frightful manners," she said to Professor Nod.

"Not at all," said Nod. "I meant to tell you about that friendly Tibetan greeting, but it slipped my mind. It wouldn't hurt if you all stuck your tongues out a bit, too." Ooola wished the other foundlings were there to hear this. They would never believe her.

They returned to Dimchuck's tent. Professor Nod proceeded to make Ooola laugh with a vivid story about the renowned Boyarsky variation in the great Yalta Chess Match of 1919. By the climax Nod was in such a lather that he was booming out the moves at the top of his lungs. "King to bishop two!" he yelled triumphantly. Ooola was doubled over with laughter.

Dimchuck frowned deeply. "In my country young ladies are not permitted to bother important scientists. I hear this professor is involved in Very Important Work."

"This fellow is as rude as his camel," Trotwood whispered to Miss Baba.

Once the travelers relaxed, they realized just how tired they were from the day's journey. Or, as Trotwood observed, tired and hungry. Dinner was the traditional Mongolian meal of three eggs and buttered tea. They were expected to eat their eggs "Mongo fashion"—with a silver toothpick. As hungry as he usually was, Trotwood found eating eggs with a toothpick, even a silver one, to be quite frustrating.

After dinner Professor Nod and Trot settled into a long game of chess, in which Nod tried to recapture the glory of the Yalta match. The guests from Ballston Spa were offered an after-dinner drink of *koumiss*.

Trotwood swirled the bubbly fluid in his cup and took a big sniff. "What is this, er, stuff?"

"Fermented mare's milk," said Dimchuck. "You like?" With a big smile he announced, "Everybody must taste *koumiss*!" They all agreed it was a very interesting drink and politely sipped a little more.

Professor Nod was soon asleep, so Trotwood took out his bubble pipe. He blew a few fancy groupings he'd been working on at home—a figure eight and one that looked like Saturn with

28

its rings. Then he picked up a *shudraga* and strummed along to a long, winding Mongolian melody.

A peaceful camaraderie settled over the group. Ooola was becoming dreamy with fatigue and the warmth of the fire. On impulse she pulled the ribbon around her neck, held the ring up to the fire, and watched firelight glint off of its highly polished surfaces. Miss Baba motioned to Ooola to put it away quickly.

They were all so sleepy, sleepier than they'd ever been before. Miss Baba and Trotwood tried to stay awake and keep watch, but even they fell into a deep sleep.

Ooola slipped in and out of a troubled dream. In it she saw an eleven-pointed star flaming brighter than the Cliffs of Zadagag against a dark, dark sky. It glowed brighter and brighter. Suddenly its light was snuffed out.

"Would you rather hear about the kingdom of Guzzerat?" asked Professor Nod.

CHAPTER SIX

Goners in the Gobi

In the cool of the morning Miss Baba sat up slowly, holding her throbbing head in her paws. "I think that nasty-tasting *koumiss* gave me a headache, Trotwood," she said as she massaged the base of her beautiful long ears.

Trotwood considered his own head and agreed. He noticed Professor Nod slumped over by the chess board. "Well, it must have been a sight, Nod and me fast asleep over what's been called the world's most exciting game." The two gently awakened the professor.

Ooola woke slowly. It had become her habit to frequently touch the ring on the ribbon around her neck. She reached for it sleepily, then sat up with a start—*the ring was missing*!

"Miss Baba, Uncle Trot! My ring is gone!" Ooola was in a panic.

"Are you positive? You've checked everywhere?" asked Miss Baba. Ooola nodded a tearful yes to both questions. "Then let's get Dimchuck and find out who has it. They must be part of the caravan."

Miss Baba pulled aside the flap of the tent, revealing . . . nothing. The caravan was gone. They were surrounded by nothing but desert and a small pile of discarded junk.

They decided to take inventory of everything left behind by the culprits. Their things were intact, but their food was gone, and so was most of their water. Even Miss Baba's egg hat and Trotwood's licorice eye patch had been removed in the night.

"The fiends! To steal a lady's hat!" Professor Nod exclaimed.

Miss Baba sifted through the pile of trash the caravan had left behind. She found a large umbrella in poor condition, four dented cups, and, most precious of all, a *dombo* almost full of water. She poured it carefully into an old battered teapot. Then she took the pot back to the tent and melted candle wax on the spout and around the lid to prevent the water from evaporating or spilling.

Trotwood found the villains had left his compass and his telescope as well as his tuxedo. He decided not to take his tuxedo—if he were to die in the desert, he saw no need for it to be formal.

While the others collected the few things that might help them survive, Professor Nod sat and thought about the curious turn of events. "Ooola, my child, that ring of yours. After you showed it to me a few weeks ago, I came across an obscure reference to it in *The Secret History of the Mongols*. As I recall, it was something about how its owner wielded great powers, and then there was a reference to a peculiarly shaped birthmark, but there was no picture of the shape." He was rummaging through his pockets, looking at scraps of paper. "I wrote myself a note about it somewhere . . . "

Within thirty minutes they were packed up and ready to go. And with the help of Trotwood's compass, they began marching south. After several hours of climbing up and down the rocky hills and towering granite shelves, the four adventurers scaled a steep pass and found themselves looking out on the heart of the desert, a bleak and lifeless scene. Their legs felt like rubber. They were thirsty and hungry.

Miss Baba muttered, "My kingdom for a horse."

Trotwood said he would settle for a horsehair. Professor Nod hoped for the first Gobi rain in two thousand years. They were beginning to feel a little desperate.

When they reached the summit of the pass, they decided to rest on a rocky overlook. Trotwood scanned the horizon for signs of life, deftly wielding his telescope, which was complete with diopter. He saw nothing. Miss Baba, meanwhile, unplugged the wax from the precious teapot. Trot descended from his roost and sighed, "Baba, old bean, I believe we're in deep yogurt."

Professor Nod was reading *The Travels of Marco Polo*. "Polo was here in 1275," he reported. "That's a good seven-hundred-odd years ago. My, my, how time flies. Would you like to hear his impressions of the Gobi Desert?"

"Save your breath, old beast," advised Trotwood kindly.

But Nod, who seemed unaffected by their predicament, read anyway. " 'This desert is the abode of many evil spirits, which amuse travelers to their destruction with most extraordinary illusions. Any persons separated from their caravan may unexpectedly hear themselves called to by their names . . . and not knowing in what direction to advance, are left to perish.' " Professor Nod looked up from his book. "Polo is, of course,

When young Ooola could go no farther,
Trotwood carried her.

talking about mirages. Whatever you see or hear, don't wander off."

"Thank you for the lecture, Professor," said Miss Baba. "Nothing like cheering us up a bit. Do you know any poems about bleaching bones or extreme thirst?"

"Did that dampen your spirits, my dear? So sorry. Would you care to hear Marco Polo's account of his trip to the kingdom of Guzzerat?" asked Nod as Miss Baba set out the four cups and divided their water into them. The water was lukewarm and had a little rust from the teapot, but they savored every drop, knowing it was their last.

The march down from the ledge was treacherous, with steep drops appearing out of nowhere and the constant danger of rockslides. Several hours later, the group finally reached the flatlands and resumed their trek south. As Trotwood examined the terrain, it appeared as battered and dry as their empty teapot.

When young Ooola could go no farther, Trotwood carried her and Miss Baba shouldered their packs. Even Professor Nod, who seemed curiously unconcerned, was stumbling with fatigue.

"Baba, old bean, I have a dim pounding in my ears. Does that mean this is . . . the end?" croaked Trotwood, through parched lips.

Miss Baba realized she too heard a dim pounding. And so did Ooola and Professor Nod.

34

Nod squinted in concentration. "I made a mental note to remember something, and I can't, for the life of me, recall what it is."

"Unless it has to do with finding water, I'm afraid it's no longer important," said Miss Baba. All together, they collapsed on a rocky ridge as the pounding in their ears grew louder.

A herd of Mongol horses thundered up over the crest...

CHAPTER SEVEN

Tamerlane

A herd of Mongol horses thundered up over the crest of the ridge. They looked like angels with their billowing manes and tails. When the leader drew up short to avoid trampling the four huddled castaways, his mane and tail trailed to the ground.

Trotwood looked up and, in a parched whisper, said, "Look here, Nod—it's one of those mirages old Polo was talking about."

Ooola said, "I thought mirages were supposed to be oases with palm trees."

Nod tried to clear some of the grit from his throat and replied thoughtfully, "Well, according to Polo, mirages can be armies and such as well. I think a herd of horses would qualify."

Miss Baba corrected her companions. "These are real horses, and if we don't stop this blather and introduce ourselves to them soon, they're likely to leave." They staggered to their feet and addressed the leader, a muscular white stallion, who was tapping his hoof impatiently.

37

"What accident of fate has brought you to this harsh kingdom so ill prepared?" asked the stallion.

Miss Baba explained about the stolen ring with the inscription *In the Valley of Condors, grasp the Doorknob of Destiny.*

The leader looked them over carefully. He walked over to Ooola and knelt before her. He said, "I am Tamerlane, one of the ten thousand. We return to the White Stallion River, to the pastures of our birth. By your luck, or our fate, the Dolly Llama, oldest and wisest of your kind, resides there among us. She will be able to counsel you. Climb on my back and I will take you there."

The other horses were fidgeting and snorting restlessly. Ooola climbed on Tamerlane's broad white back. "But aren't you going to take my three friends?" she asked.

"*Neigh, neigh,*" cried all the horses. "It is in our bloodlines to carry those of the mark and no other."

Tamerlane eyed the white star on Ooola's chest. "Our legends foretell of a new khan," he said, "one who can turn the Doorknob of Destiny, restore prosperity, and lead the nomadic tribes to great deeds. You are the one."

"Well, let me off. If you won't take the others, I won't go either!" shouted Ooola, starting to dismount. Tamerlane stomped his foot and tossed his mane, trying to sort out this problem. The other horses snorted impatiently.

"Wait one minute," Trotwood croaked. "Tamerlane, if you would be so kind as to give me a hair from your tail, I could summon some help myself." Tamerlane gladly complied, giving Trotwood a five-foot-long hair from his tail. It shone like platinum wire in Trot's paws.

Miss Baba added, "And one other thing, Tamerlane—could you leave us something to drink?" Tamerlane directed his mares to allow Miss Baba and Professor Nod to milk them (a unique experience for the wild mares and the castaways alike). They were given enough to slake their thirst and fill the teapot.

Trotwood took a thin, velvet-lined case from his pocket and removed from it a large condor tail feather. He wound Tamerlane's magnificent hair in an intricate pattern around his paws and the feather. He then put the construction to his mouth and blew. It produced a clear, unearthly whistle, almost beyond the range of all their ears.

Professor Nod, revived a bit by the milk, said, "A very good condor call. I've known only a few individuals who had mastered such a difficult call."

Trotwood corrected the professor. "To be precise, Nod, that was a condor distress call. The time has come to call in a favor a condor of this clan owes me. I've carried that feather for years, in case a situation of this sort arose. But I needed the horse's hair to make the call. Having the feather without the hair was like having a phone booth but no change."

Miss Baba spoke to Ooola and Tamerlane about their journey, then she tucked the carpet under Ooola's arm. "My dear, we will find our own way to the Valley of Condors. This detour to the Dolly Llama could be of great help to you. Thank you, Tamerlane. Good luck, my dear, and hold tight!"

She pecked Ooola on her cheek, and Tamerlane bounded down the mountain.

"Let us be off!" cried the horses. "To the White Stallion River! To the land of our birth!" They wheeled across the desert to the west. Ooola barely had time to wave good-bye.

Already two specks appeared high over the southern horizon, moving as fast as the wind, coming from the direction of the Valley of Condors.

Trotwood took a thin, velvet-lined case from his pocket...

"If you're in trouble again, don't call us…"

CHAPTER EIGHT

Two Points of the Compass

The horses were gone as quickly as they had come, and the three travelers might have thought they had really been a mirage but for Ooola's absence, the fresh mare's milk (it tasted a lot better unfermented), and Tamerlane's hair. The specks on the horizon were getting larger. They could soon discern the movement of wings, and in no time at all two giant condors were hovering above them.

One called down, "Excuse me, poor pathetic creatures, have you seen a condor in distress hereabouts?" He spoke in a nasal hiss that sounded like fine sandpaper.

Trotwood waved to them, smiling. Once again he opened the thin case that held the condor feather. Both of the great birds, upon seeing the feather, swooped down out of the sky, landing on an outcropping of a shattered statue.

"Allow me to introduce myself," said Trot. "I am Leroy Trotwood the Third. And this tail feather was given to me by Nosmo, King of the Condors."

"Ah! Nosmo! So you did a kindness for our king. Now it is our duty to repay his debt."

The second condor turned to the first and said, "Egad! Shall we offer our services without even introducing ourselves?" His voice reminded Miss Baba of the screeching of car brakes or fingernails on a blackboard.

"Ah, yes!" said the sandpaper-voiced bird. "I am Egad. This is my brother, Hoomi. Who might you be?"

Trotwood introduced everyone and explained their plight. Egad looked the group over carefully and said, "If you had asked us to watch you die and then pick your bones clean, that would have been an easy request. We do that sort of thing all the time. But, though we are known on three continents for our strength, we could not carry such well-fed creatures as yourselves, even if we were rested and still in our first feather." Turning to his brother, Egad concluded, "For the life of me, Hoomi, I don't know what to do with them."

Hoomi considered the problem. "We cannot carry you," he screeched. "So we must find another solution. If you will await our return, we will not be long."

"Thank you. We'll be here," replied Trotwood.

In a short while Egad and Hoomi returned, leading a camel loaded with fresh supplies. "Egad! It's Dash!" exclaimed Trotwood. Sure enough, it was. And Dash's feelings about Trotwood hadn't been improved by the sudden change of plans.

"*Nichtswisser!*" spat out Dash.

"Now what is he calling me?" Trot asked the professor.

Nod considered the word. "I believe he was referring to you as some sort of simpleton, fool, dunce, or all-around ignoramus."

Hoomi had hopped over to where Trotwood was standing, holding the prized condor feather. "It was amusing to help you," said the condor, grabbing the feather. "If you're in trouble again, don't call us." Hoomi and Egad disappeared as quickly as they had appeared.

The group wasted no time boarding Dash, and they continued on their course to the Valley of Condors.

Meanwhile all that day and through the night into the following day, Ooola was carried by the strongest and swiftest of horses. The desert passed under them and gave way to steppes, where tribes of wild camels and goats grazed between toothlike outcroppings of rock.

When Ooola was tired, Tamerlane told her to entwine herself in his long flowing mane and sleep. The steady hoofbeats lulled her and filled her dreams. When she awoke, it was evening. The steppes had turned to grassy hills, golden in the last rays of sun.

Before they could see it, they could hear the steady roar of the swift, turbulent waters of the White Stallion River. At last Tamerlane and his tribe bounded over a ridge and before them lay the wide waters, bordered on either side by luxuriant green pastures.

Tamerlane reared up, neighing loudly, and Ooola slipped off his flanks. The stallion dashed off to join his fellows, while Ooola fell asleep on the soft green blanket of grass.

"This rug is a genealogy," said Dolly. "It shows that you are descended from the great chiefs of the Mongol Empire...

CHAPTER NINE

The Carpet Unraveled

Ooola awoke refreshed. She stretched and rolled over on the thick bed of grass, then caught her breath. Directly in front of her were four hooves, but they were covered with gray, matted fur. They were definitely not Tamerlane's.

She looked up into the wrinkled face and yellow eyes of Dolly Llama. Dolly stuck out her tongue. Ooola thought this very rude until she remembered it was the traditional greeting in Tibet.

"Are you Dolly Llama?" Ooola asked. "Tamerlane said you were one of my kind. I thought you'd be more of a poodle."

Dolly Llama laughed. "That's Tamerlane for you. If you're not a white horse, you're one of 'the other kind.' Those White Stallions do tend to be a bit arrogant. Would you like some breakfast, my child?" Ooola realized she was very hungry, having had only a taste of milk the day before in the desert. It seemed so long ago.

They walked a short distance to Dolly's yurt (*ger* in Mongolian), which is a traditional nomad home, a collapsible felt structure. *I hope it doesn't collapse while we're in it,* thought Ooola, but it turned out to be a very sturdy home.

Nearby, on the hillside, was a statue of Buddha at least twelve feet high, taller than Dolly's yurt. Its features were sagging, and its limbs were drooping. The statue seemed to be melting slowly in the sun. Dolly offered an explanation.

"This Buddha was sculpted by the monks of the monastery nearby," she said. "It took them weeks to make, but it will not outlast the summer because it is sculpted entirely of yak butter. The message of the Buddha is that monuments and even a khan's dynasty will eventually disappear, that life on earth is transient.

Ooola's carpet: genealogy and document of state.

"After the last couple of days, I don't think I need a reminder of that, Dolly Llama," remarked Ooola.

"Ah, but it's so easy to forget," Dolly reminded her. "In any case, it is a Tibetan belief that the presence of God must be supported by our own efforts. Now, how would you like some buttered moon cakes and a nice big bowl of barley soup?"

The *ger*'s interior was sparsely furnished, with cooking pots stored in brightly colored chests and a small stove that burned wood and camel chips. Dolly settled down to read the carpet while Ooola greedily ate her food.

"This rug is a genealogy," said Dolly. "It shows here that you are a descendant of Chingis Khan and Kublai Khan, the great chiefs of the Mongol Empire who united the tribes eight hundred years ago. They spread their influence across Asia, even into Europe. This rug is a document of state. I, in fact, saw it in the hands of your grandfather when I was about your age. And now, the history not in your rug.

"When the monarchy of Mongolia was overthrown," Dolly continued, "your father, the crown prince, and your mother fled for their lives. Stowed away on a steamer, they fell ill and perished, but it was rumored that their infant daughter reached the shores of North America and safety, wrapped in this rug. That infant daughter was you, Ooola. Your proper name is Princess Ooola Oblongata, of a long and fearless lineage. And you alone have inherited the right to wield the Doorknob of Destiny. Besides, you look very much like your father. He was a good friend of mine."

Ooola smiled at the revelation. It was the first information she had ever had about her parents. "Tell me more about my family, Dolly."

"Your father was a khan. Your mother was an Oblongata...."

Dolly took a small portrait and some clothes out of one of the chests. "Here is a picture of your parents many years ago. And these clothes may come in handy during our cold nights," she said. "They were your mother's." Ooola tried them on. Dolly continued, "It was a difficult time, a time of chaos and revolt. Your father was a Khan. Your mother was an Oblongata. Two proud, strong families with long histories. But I'm afraid those stories must wait for another time. There is a more urgent matter to discuss: the Doorknob of Destiny."

Ooola asked, "But what is the Doorknob of Destiny? And why did someone go to such trouble to steal my ring, Dolly?"

Dolly replied, "Your ring *is* the Doorknob of Destiny. It's a petrified condor egg set in a silver eleven-pointed star, the symbol of the khan. By the way, did you ever count the points of the birthmark on your chest?"

Ooola looked in Dolly's mirror. *One, two, three, four, five, six, seven, eight, nine, ten, eleven.* "So that's what Tamerlane and Professor Nod meant when they were talking about 'the mark of the khan.' "

"Precisely," said Dolly. "Now, the ring is more sought after than even the true princess, because, as legend has it, the ring is the keystone to the door of a vast underground cavern that houses the enormous wealth of the khans. There is an entrance to the cavern in the place where your caravan was headed, the Valley of Condors. This cavern is guarded night and day by a tribe of nomads who consider it their sacred duty. They camp there, waiting for the new khan."

Dolly took a sip of tea. She continued, "The ring has been in your family for fifteen generations. But for the last hundred years its whereabouts have been unknown. Some say the ring never existed, that it is a legend. Yet it was stolen from you not more than two days ago."

Tears welled up in Ooola's eyes. "But I lost it. How on earth will I ever get it back?"

Dolly drew an eleven-pointed star in the dirt floor of the yurt with her hoof. Then she drew a condor egg in the middle. After a moment, she looked up at Ooola and said, "Your destiny lies in the Valley of Condors. Tamerlane will take you there. The ring is yours. It will come to you when the time is right.

"Of course," Dolly Llama added with a shrug, "I've been wrong before."

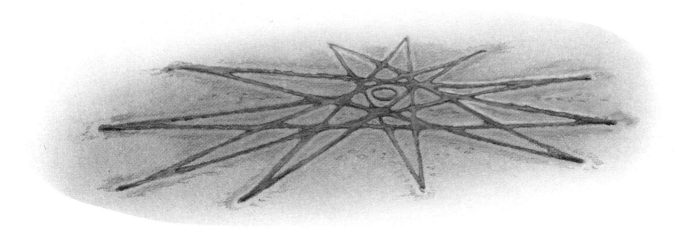

The terrain grew increasingly rugged as their destination drew near...

CHAPTER TEN

The Valley of Condors

Tamerlane had bathed in the White Stallion River. His coat and mane glowed in the sun. If possible, he looked twice as impressive to Ooola as he had in the desert. Especially when he bowed before her.

"My princess, Dolly Llama tells me we are to leave immediately for the Valley of Condors. Are you strong enough to travel?"

Ooola would have liked nothing better than to sleep for a week. Instead, she lifted herself up on Tamerlane's broad back. With Dolly Llama's blessing, off they galloped. They followed the green valley of the White Stallion River for much of the day, then veered off into the heart of the Gobi. On their ride south Ooola noticed piles of stones, some with words and symbols carved into them. She asked Tamerlane their meaning.

"The *obos*?" Tamerlane replied. "I've never given them much thought, because I never lose my way. But others use them as road markers. The monks carve prayers on stones and leave them at each *obo*. Over the centuries, I suppose, they've become shrines. Now you see travelers leaving ribbons, coins, or scraps of paper with messages on them."

Ooola had an idea. When they saw another *obo*, she stopped Tamerlane. On the pile of stones she left a tuft of her fur bound in a platinum horse's hair from Tamerlane's mane. If Miss Baba, Trotwood, and Professor Nod were to follow, they would know she had been there. (Luckily there were few *obos* and they were far apart, or Ooola and Tamerlane might have been half-bald before they reached the Valley of Condors.)

With Ooola clinging to his mane, Tamerlane galloped past deep volcanic vents and hot springs. Pencil-thin columns of basalt rock jutted out of the ground. The terrain grew increasingly rugged as their destination drew near.

They entered a deep gorge between two of the Three Beauties, the tallest of the surrounding peaks. Ooola heard a booming. "Is someone playing a huge drum, Tamerlane?" she asked.

"Neigh, my princess, the volcanoes are booming. Some say the Three Beauties are sisters and that this is how they speak with one another."

As Ooola looked up toward the three peaks she felt she was being watched. But not by the three sisters. For thousands of years the condors had built their nests on the towering cliffs surrounding the gorge. By now all of them had heard the rumors spread by Egad and Hoomi of the new heir to the throne of the khans. Hundreds of sharp eyes were intent upon the first khan to visit their valley in almost one hundred years.

Steam belched from the enormous, gaping mouth of a subterranean cave. The entrance was covered with paw and hoof prints.

"This must be it!" exclaimed Ooola.

"Then you must proceed on foot," said Tamerlane. "My kind has never entered the Cave of Destiny." He knelt for her to dismount.

Ooola walked into the cave alone, and she felt very small indeed. The entrance had a guard post, but no guard was to be

seen. She continued along the wall, in the shadows, until she
came to a vast cavern filled with flickering torches and the voices
of perhaps a thousand chanting nomads. All eyes were turned
toward an outcropping of rock above their heads, a natural
balcony blazing with torchlight. Ooola summoned her courage
and entered the cavern.

A young, bejeweled mongrel stepped out onto the balcony...

CHAPTER ELEVEN

The Eleventh Hour

A young, bejeweled mongrel stepped out onto the balcony of stone, followed by none other than Dimchuck the Camel Driver. The young one stretched out her paws to the crowd, which began chanting, "Kookla Khan! Kookla Khan!"

Something on her right paw twinkled and gleamed. Ooola felt faint. It was the Doorknob of Destiny!

"My ring!" Ooola cried, not stopping to think.

The vast cavern went silent. All eyes turned to Ooola. Dimchuck, who looked like he had seen a ghost, screamed, "IMPOSTOR! IMPOSTOR! Seize her. Bind her. Put her in irons!" The crowd swelled around Ooola. Two nomads grabbed her paws. Glaring down from the balcony, Dimchuck realized that Ooola's fur was covered with a thick layer of dust from her travels. In the dim torchlight the dust covered her eleven-pointed star birthmark.

"She has no star! She is an *impostor*!" Dimchuck cried out.

Ooola looked down and saw nothing but dust. She tried to free a paw and wipe the dust off her eleven-pointed star. But the more she struggled, the tighter her guards held her and the angrier the crowd became. The din of their voices drowned out her protests.

Before she knew it, she was bound and bundled into an ancient cage hanging to one side of the balcony. From there she had a full view of the cavern, of Kookla's coronation, and of the bursts of steam that belched in regular intervals from the yawning crack beneath her.

"Interesting pile of rocks," said the always inquisitive Trotwood. "They're mostly flat, with patterns chiseled into them. Do you suppose we've discovered a matched set of prehistoric china? That would be quite a find." Trotwood picked up a few flat stones from an *obo* as Dash walked on with Miss Baba and Professor Nod on his two humps.

Dash, still angry about being stolen by the condors, replied, "Is everyone in your country stupid, or are you an exception?"

"You're as witty as curdled custard," replied Trot. "Say, that's not a compliment in Mongolian, is it?"

As the battle of insults escalated, Miss Baba looked more closely at the *obo*. "Down, Dash! Down!" she cried. Something on the *obo* had caught her eye. She ran over to the pile of rocks and picked up a small tuft of dusty black fur bound neatly with a platinum horsehair.

"Ooola and Tamerlane have passed this way!" she exclaimed.

Dash, who liked Miss Baba as much as he disliked Trotwood, furrowed his brow. "Begging your pardon, ma'am, about that Ooola creature, you might want to know, well, it's probably not important. It's just something I overheard. Probably of no interest . . ."

"For goodness' sake, Dash," interrupted Miss Baba, "if you know something, please tell us immediately."

Dash cleared his throat. "Ahem. I overheard a great deal before those buzzards stole me. There was a plot to steal Ooola's ring. I say 'was' because they were successful. If that's what you want to call it. The ring is now in the clutches of that goat's bladder, Dimchuck, and a fat false princess, Kookla Khan.

"I saw Dimchuck painting an eleven-pointed star on her chest. And why would they do such a thing? I can tell you why. It's a plot to steal the treasure . . ."

56

Professor Nod was listening intently. "Treasure? Isn't that just a myth? Could there really be a treasure in the Valley of Condors?"

Dash was rather enjoying being the center of attention. "Most certainly," he said, puffing up his chest to look important. "The ring is the keystone, no, the link, no . . . the doorknob, yes, that's it—the doorknob to the Door of Destiny. Behind it lies the lost treasures of the khans. I shouldn't say lost, because they seem to know where it is. They just need the ring. Or, should I say, needed the ring. They must have it now."

They proceeded as quickly as Dash's swaying gait could carry them, with Trotwood jogging alongside, trying to recognize Tamerlane's unshod prints from those of the caravan. Dash hissed, "Hurry, you турист!"

"Nod?" called out Trotwood.

"He called you a tourist in Russian," replied the professor, who by now was used to the routine.

Near the mouth of the cave, Trotwood saw two sets of prints diverge. "Tamerlane turned here and knelt, and Ooola went into the cave alone!" At the cave mouth they found Ooola's pack, with the clothes Dolly had given her, wrapped in the carpet.

Miss Baba began to fear Ooola was in for some real trouble. But she could never have envisioned the barbaric sight that met their eyes when, at last, they entered the torchlit chamber. Poor Ooola was suspended over the steaming crack in the rocky floor of the cavern. Miss Baba pressed on into the crowd.

The ceremony was going slowly because of the great number of traditional songs and prayers and the pageantry of the nomad chieftains paying their respects to the new princess-to-be. As Miss Baba and Trotwood, followed by Nod and Dash, edged toward the front of the crowd, the attendants to the false princess carried out a huge vat.

Poor Ooola was suspended over the steaming crack...

The crowd went wild. "Anoint the princess. Anoint the princess with *koumiss* before she is crowned! It is written!"

Before Kookla knew it, she was doused with the huge vat of *koumiss.* Sneezing and sputtering, Kookla reached out for something to dry her eyes and caught hold of Dimchuck's beard. To the surprise of everyone in the cavern, the beard came off in Kookla's paw.

The attendants hurriedly dried Kookla off, and again, to the surprise of the entire cavern, something else was amiss. Kookla's eleven-pointed star was no longer on her chest.

"We have been deceived!" cried the Mongol nomads as they unsheathed their swords and waved them menacingly.

"Hurry, Trotwood!" called Miss Baba as they pushed forward through the heavily armed crowd.

"Things are getting ugly, aren't they?" Trot said cheerily. "The chaos is a perfect diversion for freeing Ooola."

The four rescuers stopped short of the gaping, steaming crack. Miss Baba motioned to Dash. "Dash, let Trotwood stand on your hump and pry open the cage!"

"*Wang ba dan!*" Dash muttered under his breath, but he allowed Trot to climb his back.

Ooola was shaken but unhurt. By now she was sopping wet from the jets of steam rushing up at her. The dust had been steam-cleaned off her, and now her star shone brightly. The nomads stopped their swordplay and stared in wonder and confusion.

"If you need further proof, it's all here," said Miss Baba, unrolling Ooola's carpet. Miss Baba's attention then turned to the false princess and Dimchuck, now beardless. "Well, if it isn't Miss Uptigrue, Professor Nod's assistant! I should have known no one here would share your taste in literature. So that's how you knew about Ooola's ring."

"Say, weren't you the Chinese conductor on the train?" exclaimed Ooola.

Conductor/Uptigrue/Dimchuck was beside herself. "I only wanted the treasure to help Professor Nod in his Very Important Work. I was going to return for him as soon as the ceremony was over. You were never in any real danger. Professor Nod knows the water level in the Gobi is quite close to the surface, only a meter down at most . . ."

"*That's* what I was trying to remember yesterday in the desert!" said the professor, his expression brightening. Miss Baba and Trotwood looked at Nod in disbelief. "Dreadfully sorry," he added. "I suppose that information might have come in handy out there."

"Put the false princess and the false beard in the cage!" screamed the enraged Mongols.

"No!" said Ooola, standing in front of the cowering impostors. "Miss Uptigrue and Kookla will be spared by the mercy of the Khan!" she shouted, surprising everyone, including herself, with her authority.

Miss Uptigrue collapsed at Ooola's feet and blubbered, "Spare my niece, Kookla. I convinced her it was a harmless deception. I'm sorry she ate your eyepatch and your egg. It's my fault. Do what you may with me. I'm just glad the professor is safe."

Professor Nod looked touched. "Marva, my dear, I had no idea . . ." he said.

Princess Ooola Oblongata

Meanwhile, Ooola had ascended the stairs to the balcony, where the attendant returned her ring with a great deal of pomp and ceremony. With the Doorknob of Destiny firmly in place, she went to the huge slab of a door. She was led to the notch, where she inserted the ancient condor egg and, to everyone's delight, the massive stone swung open. A mirage-like landscape of treasure was revealed—acres of the rarest black pearls, enough golden armor to outfit an army, diamond-tipped platinum arrows, shields dripping red with rubies. The riches went back out of the torchlight, deep into the cavern.

Ooola imagined the glory of the khans. Palaces covered with gold, servants catering to one's every need, and in the place of the ancient emperors she saw herself on the throne. But that fantasy gave way to thoughts of all that could be done with the treasure. Help for the needy, schools, hospitals, museums, the end of famine and disease, and so on. And she could have a hand in doing these good deeds. *Not bad for a teenage orphan*, she thought.

Her reverie was broken by a nomad guard. "My princess, er, excuse me for bothering your highness, but there are several thousand very angry white stallions and fierce condors outside the cave inquiring as to your health. Perhaps if you could talk to them, they would refrain from tearing us limb from limb . . . as they have threatened to do," he added hastily.

The guard kissed her paw and knelt with his head to his knee.

Ooola was pleased that the tribes of the Stallion and the Condor would come to her rescue. *A bit late*, she thought, *but no one's perfect.* As she turned to go to the mouth of the cave, she was inundated with warm slime. *Was it an avalanche? A mudslide? Was the volcano erupting? Will I not survive after all that has happened?* thought Ooola from under the goop.

It was only a fresh vat of *koumiss*, and in an instant the torrent had passed, leaving her once again wet and clammy. The nomad attendants had been determined to anoint a princess. They stood beside her looking very pleased.

Ooola slogged to the mouth of the cavern and into the fading daylight. An army of hooved and taloned warriors cheered. "Hail to the princess! Long live Princess Ooola Oblongata, the great khan!" rang out in neighs and screeches and hisses. If any of the terrified nomads had a lingering doubt about Ooola's authenticity, this put it to rest.

Ooola put one more matter to rest. "I am proud to be the heir to the great family of the khans. But the time has passed when Mongolia needs a princess. I am Ooola, friend of the tribes of the Mongols, the nomads, the Condors, and the Stallions. And friend is what I want to be called."

And so "Friend Ooola" she was, to all the many and diverse tribes of the wild, untamed Gobi.

Curtain
Call

The return to Ulan Bator was a difficult, three-day trek by caravan. But for Ooola, Miss Baba, Trotwood, Professor Nod, the weepy Miss Uptigrue, and Dash, it seemed as tame as it could be.

The group returned just in time for the final performance of the Traveling Theatre's *Aïda* in the giant Mongolian State Opera House. As they slipped in through the back, Trotwood was quickly explaining the plot of the opera. "It's a tragic love triangle about the daughter of the king of Ethiopia, who is now a slave in the court of Egypt, a young general in the Egyptian army, and the jealous princess of Egypt. Very sensitive."

However, under the watchful eye of Animal Maria, the plot seemed to have thickened a little, into a performance in four courses: Aïda the Salad (which was booed), Aïda the Soup (which went over better), Aïda the Entree (which was well received, especially the spaghetti with meatballs), and Aïda the Dessert (which got at least five encores). Ooola's understudy, Lucille, did a magnificent job as the Ethiopian waitress.

Trotwood felt that Animal Maria's direction had made the opera even more powerful than he had remembered it. He did miss the battle scenes, but the part she added about the blueberry pie sandwiches moved him to tears. He went backstage and congratulated every one of the foundlings for their enormous success. The reviews that appeared in *Mongolpress* were gratifyingly enthusiastic, too.

The next morning, as the group packed and prepared to leave, Ooola told them of her decision to stay in Mongolia. Ooola gave her fellow foundlings a *shatar* set as a good-bye present and took everyone's picture with her birthday camera.

Miss Baba unpacked one bag, taking out a Mongolian book called *The Poetry of Good Wishes*. On the flyleaf Miss Baba wrote: "To Friend Ooola, from the Tribe of Miss Baba's Animal Academy. Love, Miss B."

They said their good-byes with promises to write often. Miss Baba watched proudly from the back of the train as Ooola waved good-bye on the platform. The ring on her paw didn't look so big anymore.

In fact, it looked just the right size.

GLOSSARY

Aïda: One of the world's great operas. Written in 1871 by Giuseppe Verdi, this tragic love triangle set in the time of the pharaohs, the great Egyptian rulers of two thousand years ago, is considered a favorite by virtually every opera company in the world.

Arabic: Language of the Arabs, today spoken in many parts of northern Africa and the Middle East.

Ballston Spa: A quiet little New York town between Albany, the capital, and Saratoga Springs. In fact, it was founded as a suburb of Saratoga Springs by Eliphalet Ball in the late 1700s. It's also a spa—a place people visit to take mineral baths that are supposed to be good for them.

Beijing: The capital of the People's Republic of China, also called Peking. It's in northeastern China and has a population of about seven and a half million people.

Camel: Some wild, some beasts of burden capable of going two months without water. A two-humped camel such as Dash is a Bactrian camel and native to Asia. The dromedary is the one-humped camel of North Africa.

Chingis Khan: The conqueror of most of Asia and eastern Europe, which is a really *big* empire. He lived from 1162 to 1227. (It's also spelled Genghis Khan, though Chingis is the more authentic pronunciation.)

Customs: This word can mean *traditions* and *practices*. But when one crosses a national border, it means something different. *Going through customs* means having one's luggage checked for illegal items by a customs inspector.

Del: Traditional Mongolian dress. Worn by men and women like a coat, it is often made of leather, wool, and fur, is ankle-length, and has very long sleeves.

Dialect: The way people from a certain *part* of a country speak the language. People in Mississippi might have a different way of speaking than people in Massachusetts, but they can understand each other, because it's still the same language.

Diopter: An instrument used to estimate the size or elevation of distant objects. Trotwood has one with his telescope.

Dogasaurus: The "missing link" between ancient dinosaurs and modern-day dogs. No one's ever found one, but we're keeping our fingers crossed.

Dombo: A small covered pail used to hold beverages, like tea or *koumiss*. It is usually highly ornamented.

Four Horseshoes and a Feather: The seal of the khans' postal service, which was like the Pony Express in America. The horseshoes mean "urgent message." The feather means "fly, fly."

Gobi: A huge desert in southern Mongolia, about the size of Texas. It's scattered with rocks, thorny plants, and thirty-two-million-year-old fossilized dinosaur eggs. Also, in Mongolian, the word *gobi* means rocky plain—any rocky plain.

The Great Wall of China: A complex of walls, two thousand miles long, built about two thousand four hundred years ago to keep out Mongol invaders. As Miss Baba has pointed out, it's the only structure built by the earth's inhabitants that can be seen from the moon.

Guzzerat: A kingdom of India at the time of Marco Polo.

Koumiss: Fermented mare's (or camel's) milk that Mongol nomads drink.

Kublai Khan: The grandson of Chingis Khan, who lived from 1215 to 1294. He changed the Mongols from roaming warriors to people who lived in homes, owned and cultivated land, and built cities.

Lama: A great teacher and spiritual leader. In Tibet this title is given only to monks of high rank.

Llama: A large woolly-haired animal native to South America. Dolly Llama, in her youth, found her way to Mongolia.

Marco Polo: An Italian explorer who lived from 1254 to 1324 and was among the first Europeans to visit the empire of the great Kublai Khan. He wrote a book about his travels. A lot of people found his stories so unbelievable that he was put in jail for a short time.

Mongolia (Mongolian People's Republic or MPR): A country in east-central Asia, between Russia and China. Its population is about two million, most of them concentrated in or near the country's few cities, most notably Ulan Bator. Its official language is Russian, but there's also a traditional Mongolian language.

Mongolian Horses: Small, very strong, stocky ponies with characteristically enormous manes and tails. They endure great hardships and can run all day. Mongolians love their horses. They invented the saddle and may have been the first horsemen in history. See Shudraga.

"My kingdom for a horse!": William Shakespeare wrote this in the play *Richard III*. When the evil king has lost his last battle, he screams this out (Act V, scene IV, line 7).

Nichtswisser: German (a language which is commonly spoken in Mongolia) for know-nothing, simpleton, fool, dunce, or all-around ignoramus.

Obo: A pile of stones used as a road marker and/or a shrine. Many of these stones have prayers carved into or written on them.

Oud: A musical instrument, a member of the lute family, played in much of Asia and parts of Africa.

Pfister blossoms: We're not quite sure what these are. Marva Uptigrue picks them down by the Mohawk

River. From the odor of them, we suspect they're related to skunk cabbage.

Poetry of Good Wishes: A traditional form of Mongolian literature known as Yurol, along with Mag Toal, poetry of praise.

Pterodactyl: A flying dinosaur with a twenty-foot wingspan.

"San bainoo": "Hello" in Mongolian, the traditional language of Mongolia.

Sanskrit: The ancient language of Hindu India.

Saskatchewan: A province of western Canada.

Scooting shimmy: A starlike decoration that Chef Tetelli taught Animal Maria how to make.

The Secret History of the Mongols: A book of ancient legends mixed with the history of Chingis Khan. It's an epic chronicle that had to be kept secret when it was first written, because the king at that time was afraid its tales of the great khan might incite people to overthrow his reign.

Shatar: The Mongolian word for the game of chess, popular in Mongolia.

Shudraga: A three-stringed banjolike instrument of Mongolia. A variation of the *shudraga*, called the *morin khour*, which has a legendary origin: an ancient noble is said to have loved his horse so much that when it died he made an instrument out of its bones and hair.

Steppes: A plain of grassland without trees.

Tamerlane: Mongolian conqueror of much of southern and western Asia. Ruler of Samarkand (now a city of Soviet Asia) 1336–1405. Also the title of a great play by Christopher Marlowe.

The Three Fateful Hills: A popular opera in Mongolia about a wealthy landowner who tries to marry the heroine against her will, but the young woman is rescued just in time by her true love.

Tibet: An area of southwestern China with some of the world's highest mountains.

Trilobites: Big, buglike water creatures that lived during the same time as the dinosaurs.

Ulan Bator: The capital city of Mongolia.

Urga: The old name for Ulan Bator, when it was the religious center of Mongolia.

Wattles: Fleshy flaps of skin found on the neck or head of birds, lizards, and goats.

Yurt: The Russian word for a large, sturdy tentlike home made of poles covered with felt, skins, or often canvas. The Mongol word for *yurt* is *ger*.

BIBLIOGRAPHY

Across China by Peter Jenkins. New York: Morrow, 1986.

Area Handbook for Mongolia by Trevor N. Dupuy and others. Washington, D.C.: U.S. Government Printing Office, 1970.

Development of the Mongolian National Style Painting "Mongol Zurag" in Brief by N. Sultern. Ulan Bator, Mongolia: State Publishing House, 1986.

China by Rail by Patrick and Maggy Whitehouse. New York: Vendome Press, 1988.

Fine Arts in Contemporary Mongolia. Ulan Bator, Mongolia: State Publishing House, 1971.

"Journey to Outer Mongolia," *National Geographic*, Vol. 121, No. 3, March 1962, p. 289.

The Modern History of Mongolia by C. Bawden. New York: Praeger, 1968.

The Mongol Empire by Michael Prawdin. London: George Allen and Unwin, 1961.

Mongolia, Unknown Land by Jorgen Bisch. New York: Dutton, 1963.

Mongolian Arts and Crafts by N. Tsultem. Ulan Bator, Mongolia: State Publishing House, 1987.

National Costumes of the M.P.R. by L. Sonomtseren. Ulan Bator, Mongolia: State Publishing House, 1967.

The New Encyclopaedia Britannica Vol. XII by Helen Hemingway Benton. London, 1981.

Nomads and Commissars: Mongolia Revisited by Owen Lattimore. New York: Oxford University Press, 1962.

Postage Stamps of the M.P.R. by G. Radnazar. Ulan Bator, Mongolia: State Publishing House, 1984.

Riding the Iron Rooster by Paul Theroux. New York: G. P. Putnam's Sons, 1988.

Tent Life in Siberia by George Kennan. Salt Lake City, UT: Peregrine Smith Books, 1986.

"Time Catches up with Mongolia," *National Geographic*, Vol. 167, No. 2, February 1985, p. 242.

The Travels of Marco Polo by Marco Polo, edited by Edward W. Marsden. New York: Dorset Press, 1987.

Winslow at Tula Gol, Mongolia

PHOTO BY PETER ROSE

Richard in Ballston Spa, New York

Winslow Pinney Pels is a freelance illustrator for publishing, advertising, and the performing arts. Other books illustrated by Ms. Pels include *The Magic Fish, Stone Soup, Beauty and the Beast, Hansel and Gretel*, and Miss Baba's first adventure, *The Caribbean Foul Ball Caper*, which she also cowrote.

Richard Pels is associate creative director of a New York advertising agency. He has a B.A. from the University of Rochester and an M.F.A. in creative writing from the University of Oregon. He is also a published poet and coauthor of *The Caribbean Foul Ball Caper*.

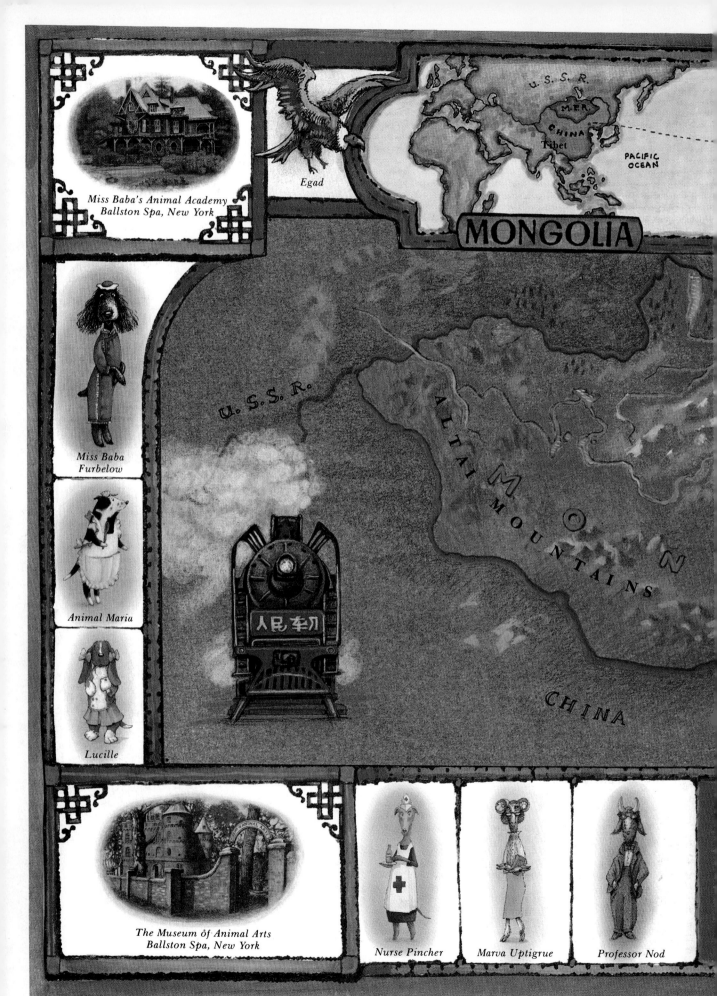

Miss Baba's Animal Academy
Ballston Spa, New York

Egad

U. S. S. R.

M.P.R.

CHINA

Tibet

PACIFIC
OCEAN

MONGOLIA

U. S. S. R.

ALTAI MOUNTAINS

MON

CHINA

人民李刀

Miss Baba
Furbelow

Animal Maria

Lucille

The Museum of Animal Arts
Ballston Spa, New York

Nurse Pincher

Marva Uptigrue

Professor Nod